The "AWFUL MESS" MYSTERY

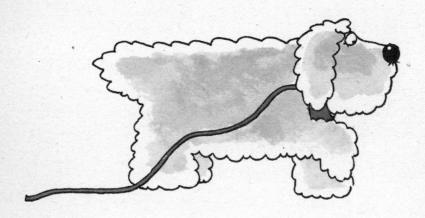

Written by Adrian Robert
Illustrated by Paul Harvey

Troll Associates

Library of Congress Cataloging in Publication Data

Robert, Adrian.
    The ''awful mess'' mystery.

    Summary: Four friends search for a missing
bracelet to get Katie out of a really awful mess.
    1. Children's stories, American. [1. Mystery and
detective stories] I. Harvey, Paul, 1926-   ill.
II. Title.
PZ7.R5385Aw   1985   [E]   84-8724
ISBN 0-8167-0402-3 (lib. bdg.)
ISBN 0-8167-0403-1 (pbk.)

The "AWFUL MESS" MYSTERY

"Oh...I'm in an absolutely awful mess," Katie wailed.

Robin and Jeff and Mark looked at each other. They knew the kind of messes Katie got into.

"Is it worse than the time you spilled the green paint on the cat?" Mark asked.

"Is it worse than when you let Rags drag the laundry through the mud?" asked Robin.

"Is it as bad as the time you lost your mom's car keys?" asked Jeff kindly.

"It's worse than *anything*. It's an absolutely awful, terrible *mess!*"

They were in the clubhouse in Jeff's back yard. It was really an old playhouse that looked like a little log cabin. Robin and Jeff and Mark and Katie thought they were too old for playhouses. But they weren't too old for clubs. This was their first meeting.

The club didn't have a name yet. They didn't even know what kind of club it was. They were supposed to decide that now. But first, it looked like they had to straighten out Katie's mess. And before they could do that, they had to find out what it was.

When Katie was excited she talked in
circles. Her eyes got big. She shook her head.
All she did was say how awful things were.
She forgot to say why.

PRIVATE
DO NOT
ENTER

"Sit down and take a deep breath," said Jeff.

"Have some lemonade," said Robin. She passed Katie a paper cup.

"Have some cookies," said Mark. "Cookies always help." He handed Katie a box of peanut-butter cookies. "Peanuts are brain food," he said.

Katie took the cookies and the lemonade.
She took a deep breath. Then she munched
and munched while everybody waited.

"Katie," Jeff said at last. "The club hasn't got all day. What's the absolutely awful mess?"

Katie sat up straight and blew her hair out of her eyes. "You know that bracelet my Dad gave my Mom for her birthday last week?"

Everybody nodded. Katie had helped her dad pick it out. She had talked about the bracelet for days. Knowing Katie, the other club members now feared the worst.

Katie took a deep breath. "I lost it!"

Jeff and Mark and Robin stared at her.

"You *lost* your mom's new bracelet?" Mark asked.

"How did you do that?" Jeff asked.

"Why did you have it?" Robin wanted to know.

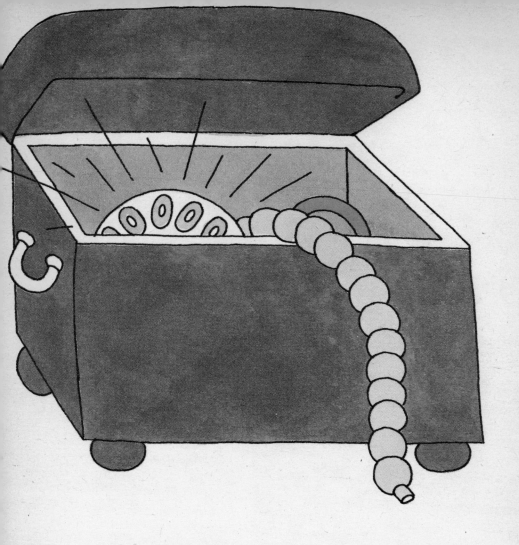

Katie swallowed hard. "It was so pretty," she said. "I wanted to see how it looked on me. We're picking officers for the club today. I thought if I got to be president I'd ask Mom to lend me the bracelet. It would look great to wear if we had a ceremony."

14

Nobody wanted to say Katie was too careless to be a president.

"You borrowed it," said Robin. "And then you forgot you had it on." Robin knew Katie pretty well.

Katie nodded miserably. "Rags got loose, and I had to chase him around the block.

Then I bought an ice cream at the ice-cream
truck. Then Mom made me clean up my
games and stuff. I didn't notice my arm was
bare till I was coming here. I hoped you guys
would help me find the bracelet before Mom
finds out it's gone."

Jeff and Mark and Robin looked at each other. There was only one thing to do. Jeff rapped on the table. "The business before this club is to find Katie's mother's bracelet," he said. "Meeting is adjourned until we do."

First, they had to decide where to look.

"What did you do when you had the bracelet on?" Jeff asked.

"I *told* you!" Katie said. "I chased Rags. I bought ice cream. I cleaned up my toys. I came over here."

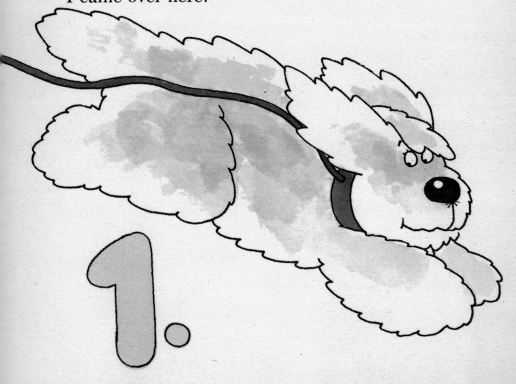

"Let's look for it at your house first,"
Robin said. "That's closest."

Katie nodded. "Maybe we can find it
before Mom does," she said.

Katie's mother was vacuuming the dining

room. "Don't track dirt on the rug!" she
warned. "In fact, don't get dirty. Dad's
taking us out for dinner. Katie, you can wear
your new blue dress. I'll wear my new
bracelet."

Katie and her friends tried not to look at each other.

"Let me run the vacuum for you, Mrs. Stone," Jeff said. "I know how. I'll be very careful." He thought he might be able to find the bracelet in the rug.

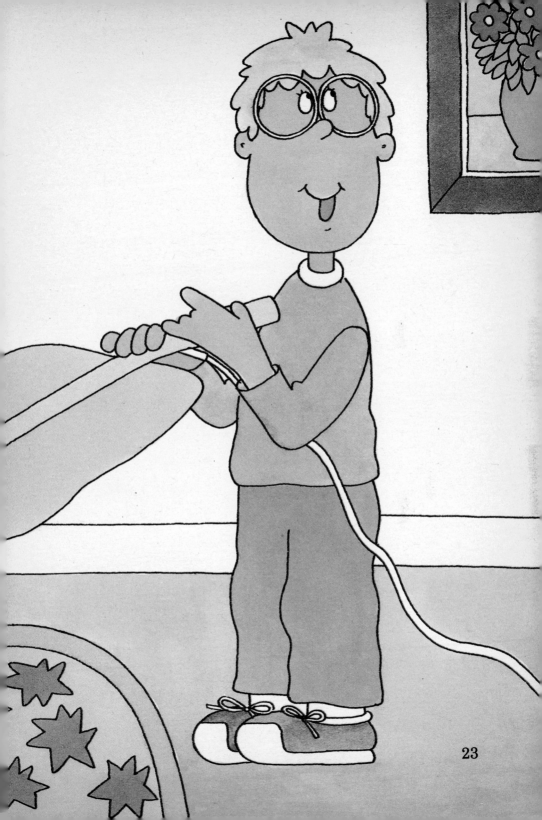

23

Katie, Mark, and Robin went up to
Katie's room. They took everything out of the
toy chest, then put it all back again. The
bracelet wasn't there. They went down to the
playroom and took all the games off the
shelves. The bracelet wasn't there, either.

"I picked up books in the living room,"
Katie remembered. So Mark and Katie and
Robin looked there, too.

Mrs. Stone found Mark with his head
under the couch. "What *are* you children
looking for?" she asked.

"Clues," Mark said in a deep voice. He hoped she would think they were playing a detective game.

"Well, see if you can find my gold earring," Mrs. Stone said. "I dropped it somewhere."

Mark soon found the earring under a chair cushion. But he didn't find the bracelet.

Jeff joined him. "It's not in the dining room," he whispered. "I even looked in the vacuum bag. We'd better try somewhere else."

Katie hooked a leash on Rags' collar. "Let's take him around the block where I chased him," she said. "Rags can be a police dog and search for clues."

Rags didn't look like a police dog. He looked like a floor mop on legs. But he dragged Katie back around the block. The others ran after them. Rags sniffed all the weeds and looked around all the trash cans. But nobody found a sparkling bracelet in the grass.

"Let's look where you got the ice cream," Robin said.

"I got it from the ice-cream wagon on the corner," Katie said.

The ice-cream truck wasn't there
anymore. Jeff and Mark and Katie and Robin
looked in the grass. They looked along the
curb. They looked around the big stone
where Katie sat to eat her ice cream.

It was their last hope. But there was no trace of the missing bracelet.

Katie kicked a pebble. "Thanks, guys," she said, "but it's no use. The bracelet is gone forever. I might as well go home and tell my mom."

Just then they heard the ice-cream truck
down the block. "Da-de-de-de-dum" blew the
truck's horn.

"We can ask the ice-cream man," Jeff said. "Maybe *he* saw the bracelet."

The ice-cream man shook his head. "I haven't seen any bracelets," he said. "You kids should be more careful."

Tears trickled down Katie's face. They left two paths down her cheeks. The ice-cream man felt badly for her. He reached into his case. "Maybe this will make you feel better," he said. He gave Katie an ice cream.

Katie didn't even feel like eating it.

"Go on, kid," the man urged. "It's the kind you like. Lime ice on vanilla ice cream. I remember because it took you so long to find it. You leaned into the case so far I thought you might fall in."

Robin's eyes grew bright. "Can *I* look in the case, mister?" she asked.

Robin leaned far into the case, just as Katie had. She looked all around. There were ice-cream sandwiches, orange ice, vanilla cones with chocolate coating, and chocolate cones with nuts. Sparkling crystals of ice clung to the ice cream and to the sides of the case. In the far corner, one thing sparkled even more.

Robin couldn't reach it. She bobbed up
and tugged the ice-cream man's arm.

"Please!" she said. "Please, will you get
that?"

The man looked. His eyes grew big. He
bent way over and reached in.

When he pulled his arm out of the case,
something shiny dangled from his hand.

"Is this what you're looking for, young
lady?" he asked.

"The bracelet!" Katie's face lit up.
"Oh, thank you! You just got me out of the
most awful mess!"

40

"I think your friends did," said the ice-cream man. And he gave them each an ice cream.

"*Now* can we have our club meeting?" asked Jeff.

First, they stopped at Katie's house. Katie
gave her mother the bracelet and told her
what had happened. Mrs. Stone looked as if
she didn't know whether to be mad or happy.

Then they went back to the clubhouse. Jeff rapped for order. "We have a lot to do," he said. "We have to pick officers. We have to pick a name. And we have to decide what kind of club this is."

Mark smiled. "We've already found that out," he said. "We're a club that solves absolutely awful messes. We're detectives!"

He took Jeff's paints and made a sign.
It said, DETECTIVES, INC. AWFUL
MESSES SOLVED.

Jeff was made president. Robin was made vice president. Mark was made secretary because he could print so well.

"But what am I going to be?" Katie asked.

Jeff grinned. "That's easy!" he said. "You can find cases for us to solve. You're Vice President in charge of Absolutely Awful Messes!"